FURRY PURRY
BEANCAT

other

THE
WITCH'S
CAT

PHILIP ARDAGH

More
Furry Purry Beancat
adventures!

THE PIRATE CAPTAIN'S CAT

THE RAILWAY CAT

THE LIBRARY CAT

THE NINE LIVES OF
FURRY PURRY
BEANCAT

THE
WITCH'S
CAT

PHILIP ARDAGH

Illustrated by

Rob Biddulph

SIMON & SCHUSTER

First published in Great Britain in 2021 by Simon & Schuster UK Ltd

A CIP catalogue record for this book is available from the British Library.

PB ISBN 978-1-4711-8405-5
eBook ISBN 978-1-4711-8406-2

This book is a work of fiction. Names, characters, places and incidents are either
the product of the author's imagination or are used fictitiously. Any resemblance
to actual people living or dead, events or locales is entirely coincidental.

Printed and bound by CPI Group (UK) Ltd, Croydon, CR0 4YY

For Jackie Morris,
a white witch
(or enchantress)
if ever there was one
Philip Ardagh

For Pongo, Purdy and Molly
Rob Biddulph

Furry Purry Beancat found a patch of sunlight, followed her tail round in a circle three times, then settled herself down in a furry ball of purry cat. She yawned, lowered her head to the ground and pulled her beautiful fluffy tail in front of her little pink nose.

Where will I wake up next? she wondered, slowly closing her big green eyes and drifting off to sleep . . .

CHAPTER 1
WITCH!

'**W**itch!' cried a voice.

Furry Purry Beancat opened an eye. *What cheek!* she thought. *Who's disturbing my sleep?*

'Witch!' shouted another, much deeper, voice. A very large shoe whistled over Beancat's head, missing it by a (cat's) whisker!

What on earth's going on? Beancat wondered with a start. She opened the other eye, jumping up on her four white paws and dashing behind a tree.

The tree smelled of badger.

She soon discovered why.

Losing her footing, she found herself tumbling down a hole – 'MEOW!' – and her furry bottom met a badger coming the other way!

'Watch out!' snarled the badger.

'Sorry!' said Beancat, leaping up and out of the hole, the badger close behind (her behind). She instinctively knew not to mess with a badger. Though his shovel-like front claws were built for digging, he could send her flying with a single swipe,

if he wanted to. 'There's a really unfriendly crowd charging about!' she warned.

'Huh! Humans,' snarled the badger. 'Such a nuisance. Soldiers for the king. Soldiers against the king. All traipsing through here, marching and shouting, Nothing but trouble, humans.'

For and against the king? thought Beancat, storing away the information for later. *Interesting.*

They both hid behind the trunk of the tree to get a better look.

The man who'd thrown the shoe was very large and very muscly, and was leading a small rabble of men, women and children. They were simply dressed and all but one of the women wore white-cotton caps. Some

were shaking fists, others brandishing sticks or – Beancat reckoned – anything they could lay their hands on. One small boy was even waving a wooden spoon with a bite taken out of it!

Furry Purry Beancat could tell who'd thrown the shoe because the man in question was now hobbling along at the front of the crowd wearing the one shoe he had left.

'She's getting away!' yelled the grey-haired capless woman, just behind him. Her tangle of hair looked like a bird's nest.

'Oh, it's THEM,' muttered the badger. 'That big one – Thomas – is always looking for trouble. Or making it. He's almost as bad as those soldiers.'

When the huge man reached his shoe, he snatched it up and tried to pull it back on to his foot without stopping. This strange kind of one-footed hopping made him nearly fall flat on his face.

Furry Purry Beancat smiled to herself. Cats, of course, don't smile in the same way that we humans do. They may look like they have a smile on their face sometimes, but that's just the shape of their mouths. When I say that Beancat smiled, I mean on the *inside*, like when we smile. We also *feel* the joy or the fun or the happiness that made us smile in the first place. That's what Beancat's smile was: a feeling.

She quickly tried to sum up the situation from her hiding place. That was the trouble

with having nine lives. She didn't know where she was, what century it was, or just what it was she'd woken up in the middle of!

The rabble seemed to be made up of a small group of poor villagers, mainly workers by the look of them. Their clothes were straightforward and down

to earth, patched
and worn. There
was no finery
or decoration.
These weren't clothes
designed to make people look
good. They were simply clothes
to wear.

Beancat sniffed the air with
that beautiful pink nose of
hers. *Yup, these people could
do with a wash too.* She
sniffed again.

Have they EVER had a wash? she wondered.

The man the badger had called Thomas – the big man leading the way and behaving as if he were in charge – had blackened skin and he smelled of ash and molten metal. His hands, the size of hams, were hardened and thick with grime. He had a hammer tucked in his belt.

He's a blacksmith. At least he's not waving around that hammer of his! thought Beancat, only to be interrupted by another cry of, 'Witch!' from one of the mob.

'Stay out of trouble,' said the badger, not unkindly. 'If you turn up in my house uninvited again, I might swipe first

and ask questions later.'

'Sorry about that,' said Furry Purry Beancat.

'Humph,' said the big bruiser of a beast, turning and heading back down his sett, which is what a badger's burrow is called. 'Soldiers . . . villagers . . . and now strange cats!' he muttered.

He's going off to sleep, I expect, thought Beancat. *Badgers usually sleep in the day.*

Beancat had been in such a hurry to nip behind a tree to hide from the noise that she'd forgotten about the *target* of this angry mob: the one they were calling 'witch'.

Dashing through the undergrowth with an elegance only a cat can manage, it

didn't take long for her to catch up with the woman who was trying to flee her attackers. The most immediately striking thing about her was the colour of her hair (as black as night) and the amount she had of it (lots).

She certainly doesn't look like a witch, thought Furry Purry Beancat, as she ran alongside her. *But, then again, what do witches look like? She certainly smells different to the others.*

The woman's clothes were not unlike those worn by the women chasing her, but she had little pouches hanging from a belt round her waist and no cap.

Furry Purry Beancat did another one of her pink-nosed cat-sniff specials.

Herbs! The pouches are filled with all

sorts of different herbs! she realized.

The dark-haired woman would probably have been able to run faster if she hadn't been carrying a large bag – more of a small sack – over her shoulder, but Beancat could tell by the woman's look of grim determination that she wasn't planning on going anywhere without it.

She looked down and saw Furry Purry Beancat effortlessly running beside her. 'Hello, puss,' she said, 'you haven't seen my Santos, have you?' Her face was covered in a thin film of sweat, with streaks of dirt where she must have brushed against twigs and branches as she tried to escape.

So you don't know my name, thought Beancat. *You can't be my special person, after all. I wonder who Santos is?* Wherever Furry Purry Beancat woke up, *whenever* Furry Purry Beancat woke up, she always found that special person who she belonged to and who belonged to her. (Cats never really *belong* to people in the way that dogs do.)

'I just hope those poor ignorant fools

don't catch him. He's not as fast on his paws as he once was!' said the woman.

Aha! thought Beancat. What with waking to find herself in other lives with no memory of ever having been there before, she had become very skilled at gathering small snippets of information as quickly as possible to make sense of what was going on. *This Santos must be your cat. You'd hardly ask another cat about a DOG . . .*

'There she is!' a voice called out behind them.

The mob was gaining on them!

Something went flying through the air and hit the back of the fleeing woman or, to be more accurate, it hit the sack on her back and pinged off.

That was close, thought Beancat, looking back at the object lying on the ground behind them. It wasn't a shoe this time, but a broken jug.

'Give yourself up unto us, Hazel Ravenhair!' shouted Thomas the blacksmith. 'We far outnumber you!'

'You'll get a fair trial!' shouted another.

Hazel Ravenhair – for that was the name of the would-be witch with the hair as dark as midnight – snorted with indignation but didn't bother to reply. Completely unexpectedly, she dashed off to the right. Such a strange and sudden movement even took Furry Purry Beancat by surprise.

It now dawned on her that Hazel Ravenhair wasn't simply running away

in any old direction. She knew *precisely* where she was going.

'Follow me, puss,' she breathed, 'or you'll give the game away.'

Less than a minute later, the rabble reached the spot where Hazel Ravenhair and Beancat would have been. *Should* have been.

But weren't.

Everyone looked around in amazement, slashing aside the undergrowth with their sticks, looking for hiding places, peering up into the trees to see if she had scrambled up one of them.

They were nowhere to be seen.

'They've disappeared!' said Bird's-nest Hair.

'She's vanished them both away!' said a boy in wonder.

'If that ain't proof enough that she's a witch, I don't know what is,' growled their blacksmith leader, bending over to look for entrances to rabbit holes or badger setts. 'We've done what we can. It's time to call upon the witchfinder.'

CHAPTER 2
AUNT AGNES

Furry Purry Beancat blinked. Being a cat, her eyes don't need nearly as much light to see as we humans do, so she could take in her surroundings much better than Hazel Ravenhair, the would-be witch, who was squeezed in behind her, with her sack.

They were inside the trunk of a hollow tree. There wasn't much room, and it was decidedly uncomfortable, but they weren't there for fun, were they?

Beancat swivelled her ears in the dark.

She could pick up every word they were saying outside. She could hear the sticks swishing aside the undergrowth, the footsteps and talk of the witchfinder.

I don't like the sound of this witchfinder, she thought. *If ordinary people chase witches, I bet someone whose job it is to find them will be even more unkind!*

Long after the voices of her pursuers had faded into the distance, Hazel Ravenhair pushed open the door-sized piece of bark and blinked in the daylight. Furry Purry

Beancat scampered out after her. Hazel replaced the piece of bark and it blended in perfectly with the rest of the tree. There really was no way of knowing that it was anything but solid. She fluffed up some ferns in front of it.

'If you're coming with me, puss,' said Hazel, 'we'd better get going.'

Now, in case you didn't already know it, I should explain that cats understand us humans, whatever language we speak. They can't talk back – well, not in our language, anyway – but they know full well what we're up to. If you need to take a cat to the vet and they don't want to get in their basket, and you say, 'But the nice vet is going to make you better!' it's not that

they don't understand. It's just that THEY DON'T WANT TO GET IN THE BASKET.

Most cats, such as the beautiful and talented Ms Furry Purry Beancat, can speak Animal too, which means that she can talk to everything from a mouse to an elephant to a sparrow to a flying squirrel (or even a grumpy badger).

Now, there ARE humans who can have conversations with cats, but they're about as rare as hen's teeth. And if you thought, *But hens don't have teeth!* then that should give you an idea as to just how rare they are.

Often much of the conversation actually occurs *inside* the heads of the human and the cat. Furry Purry Beancat has met at least one person like that – a boy in one of

30

her other nine lives – but, of course, being Beancat, she has no memory of it.

Although Hazel Ravenhair was speaking to Furry Purry Beancat as if this beautiful fluffball of a cat could understand her, it was clear at once to Beancat that the woman couldn't understand her back.

Beancat wondered if Hazel was a witch, or if there even were such things as witches. *If so, what do witches DO?* she pondered.

She thought about this as she trotted alongside Hazel, picking her way through the forest undergrowth, being careful to stay off the paths and stopping, every once in a while, to keep an eye and ear out for anyone else.

The thing about being Beancat was, whichever of her nine lives she woke up in, there were certain general things she always knew, such as it gets dark at night, she hates water, clocks tell you the time, and that kind of thing – the general knowledge you need to get through the day without falling off a cliff. It was only the specifics – who, what, where, when, why – that were a complete mystery to her and required quick thinking on her four paws.

So what did she know about witches? Furry Purry Beancat was thinking about it so hard that she scrunched up her adorable Furry Purry Beancat face with effort, as she weaved between brambles, snuck between ferns and tiptoed between tree roots.

Okay, she thought, *witches wear pointy black hats, ride on broomsticks, make magic spells and have black cats.* Her eyes widened. *Santos must be a WITCH'S cat!*

Furry Purry Beancat studied Hazel Ravenhair as she walked beside her. For a start, she wasn't wearing a pointy black hat, and they were walking, so there was no broomstick involved . . .

Maybe the pointy black hat is more like a witch's uniform, only worn when on duty – doing spells and stuff – or at ceremonies? As for flying on a broomstick, sometimes it must be more convenient to walk, Beancat reasoned, *though a broomstick would have made for a much quicker getaway just now, without having to hide in a hollow tree!*

33

The light was beginning to fade when they reached a small wooden cottage – more of a hut or a hovel – in the very heart of the woodland, not in a clearing but right amongst the trees. Much of it was built from branches and, had you not known it was there – or had the super-sniffing ability of one Furry Purry Beancat – you might well have missed it. It wasn't so much disguised as 'blending in'.

Hazel Ravenhair knocked on the door. Not too hard, Beancat suspected, in case the whole shack came tumbling in.

'Who calls upon me at this late hour?' called a voice, as thin as paper, from inside.

'It's me, Aunt Agnes. It's Hazel!'

Beancat heard the lifting of a latch from the inside, the door opened a crack and there stood a bent-backed old lady with more lines on her face than on the bark of the hollow tree. 'Come in! Come in!' she said, opening the door wide enough for Hazel to pass through and to see out, so that her eyes could dart across the forest in the fading light. 'For a moment there, I thought a stray Roundhead might have stumbled upon my house!'

Beancat slipped into the cottage too. It was a single room. There was a table, two stools and, against the far wall, a bed with a straw mattress.

Roundhead? Who or what is a Roundhead? she wondered. *Someone with a head like a pumpkin?*

'Have there been more soldiers in the forest of late, then, Aunt Agnes?' asked Hazel Ravenhair, anxiety in her voice.

'Oh no, child,' chuckled the old woman. 'Not for two weeks since, but they were so afraid of ghosts and ghoulies that some broke ranks and may still be wandering about lost.'

Hmmm, thought Beancat. *Then a Roundhead is a type of soldier.*

'And who is this?' asked the old woman, bending down and stroking Furry Purry Beancat between the ears.

She purred.

'I do not know,' said Hazel Ravenhair. 'She appeared and has kept me company during my escape from the villagers.' She took the bag off her back and the pouches from her belt and laid them on the end of the table. 'Another lost soul, perhaps?'

'I've never met a cat who doesn't know precisely what she's doing,' said the old lady. 'And this one is very beautiful.'

I am, aren't I? thought Furry Purry Beancat, purring even MORE loudly. *How right you are.* She studied the old lady's face. *You have kind eyes*, she thought.

They're like Hazel's! She called you 'aunt' and there's certainly a family resemblance.

'Sit down! Sit down! Why are they after you, child?'

Hazel Ravenhair pulled up a stool and sat down. 'They say I have cast a spell upon Mucky John that has made him ill, Aunt Agnes.'

Agnes snorted like a snorty pig. 'When has Mucky John ever been *well*, except those times when you have treated him?'

'That's the truth,' said Hazel Ravenhair. 'When a patient is cured, they praise the Lord. If they become sicker, the blame is put upon me, but it's the first time anyone's claimed that I've somehow cast a spell upon a man!'

Beancat, meanwhile, was circling the outer edges of the room, familiarizing herself with every nook and cranny. The floor was made of hard earth, compacted solid after years underfoot. Everything was surprisingly clean.

'What ails Mucky John on this occasion?' asked Agnes, sitting opposite Hazel. She handed her a cup of water.

'Face ache and the sweats,' said Hazel.

'And your treatment?'

'Cloves for toothache, a poultice for the swollen face, and white-willow bark and elderflower for his temperature,' said Hazel.

'But?'

'His temperature has become a fever and he suffers vivid dreams.'

Hmmm, they sound more like doctors discussing a patient than a witch – or witches – casting spells, thought Beancat.

'And they all think that these dreams are somehow visions, I'll be bound?'

Hazel Ravenhair took a drink of water. 'Mucky talked of seeing Martha, his biggest sow, rising from the well, and soon it was the talk of the village that he has witnessed a vision of a great monster rising out of nowhere . . . and somehow they see this as proof of my dangerous dark magic at work!'

'Those foolish folk wouldn't know dangerous dark magic if it rose up from the depths of Hell and bit them on the bottom!' said old Agnes, with a cackle.

Hazel's face broke into a grin.

Furry Purry Beancat jumped up on to her lap. *That's the first time I've seen you smile today*, she thought. The would-be witch began to stroke her absentmindedly. She *puuuuuurred*.

Beancat hadn't simply been eavesdropping; she was still trying to make sense of this life she'd woken up in.

Hazel mentioned Mucky John's biggest sow, she thought, *and a sow's a she-pig, so he must look after pigs. No wonder he's called mucky! As for Hazel, she's some kind of healer who uses her herbs and potions to help others . . .* She thought of the angry mob who'd been chasing her through the forest. Not that they'd been grateful.

'And was it Thomas the blacksmith who shouted loudest and longest against you?' Agnes asked Hazel.

'Without question. He placed himself right at the front of the rabble,' said Hazel Ravenhair. 'Leading the charge, he was,

with his crazy-haired sister, Jane, close behind. And to think it was last summer he wanted to marry me.'

'It was *because* you refused to be his bride that he's so furious with you now,' said Agnes. 'Do you think he'd be calling you a witch if you'd agreed to marry him?'

'Do you think he'd have let me continue my work as a healer if I was his wife? Course he would not.' Hazel looked down at Beancat on her lap. 'You know, this truly is a most beautiful cat, wherever she has come from. She's so furry . . . and purry!' She began stroking Furry Purry Beancat more vigorously, right down to the tip of her tail.

'So what are your plans?' asked the old woman. 'Stay here for tonight, but what about tomorrow?'

'Tomorrow, Aunt, I shall have to get even further from the village.'

'It seems so wrong, my child. You devote your life to helping others, but it is you who is forced to flee!'

Agnes got up and returned with a wooden platter in her gnarled, twisted hands. She plonked it down in front of Hazel. On it was a heel of bread and a piece of cheese so dry that it hardly smelled cheesy at all. 'Eat,' she said.

Hazel Ravenhair didn't need asking twice. 'Thank you,' she said, and snatched up the hunk of bread and began chewing.

'I heard talk of summoning the witchfinder,' said Hazel between bites.

Agnes snorted again. 'Witchfinder? Silas Steele? A grand title for a self-important man. The self-appointed buffoon!'

Self-appointed? That means he gave himself the job, Beancat mused. *He made HIMSELF the witchfinder!*

'I was no great supporter of King Charles before he lost his head,' Agnes continued, 'but we were left to lead our lives. Since we are now ruled by Cromwell and Parliament, we've had more trouble in three years than in a lifetime. And now this Steele the witchfinder shall make matters even worse.'

Lost his head? thought Furry Beancat. *How can a king lose his head? Down the back of the sofa? Left it at the palace by mistake? It makes no sense! Oh.* Beancat shuddered. *THIS KING CHARLES MUST HAVE HAD HIS HEAD SEPARATED FROM*

HIS BODY, and this fellow Cromwell now rules with Parliament instead . . . I've woken up in dangerous times!

'Self-appointed or not, from what I've heard, Silas Steele is good at what he does—' Hazel started to say.

'Which be taking the money of folk foolish enough to pay him, then stirring up trouble for some innocent woman!' snapped Agnes. 'If Thomas the blacksmith, his sister Jane, and the others are looking for true evil, they need look no further than the witchfinder himself!'

CHAPTER 3
VELVET PELT, FLEET OF PAW

Hazel Ravenhair spent the night at her Aunt Agnes's cottage, so it made sense for Furry Purry Beancat to do the same. Agnes only had one bed so she and Hazel shared it. They kept their clothes on for warmth, and climbed under just one blanket.

Furry Purry Beancat decided to sleep on the bed too. Well, the truth be told, she decided to sleep *on* Hazel Ravenhair *on* the bed. And, to be even more accurate, she decided to sleep on Hazel's *head*. It was more comfortable that way, for her at least!

Hazel Ravenhair had other ideas and pushed her away.

'Not upon my head, puss!' she said.

The cheek of it, thought Furry Purry Beancat. *She should see it as an honour.* Then she settled down quite happily, squeezed in next to the would-be witch.

Beancat was woken the next morning by something scampering across the bed.

She opened her eyes. And there, as bold as brass – up on its hind legs and staring right at her – was a mouse.

'Well, you've certainly made yourself at home!' said the mouse.

'And who are you?' asked Beancat, doing one of those impressively large catty yawns that showed off ALL her teeth and the ribbed roof of her mouth. It was important that the mouse knew who was boss.

'I'm the one who should be asking the questions,' said the mouse.

'Are you sure?' asked Beancat. 'I'm the great big furry one with bitey teeth and scratchy claws.'

'I'm not afraid of you,' said the mouse, and it was clear that she wasn't lying. There wasn't so much as a quiver in one of her tiny mousy whiskers.

'I'm Furry Purry Beancat,' said Furry Purry Beancat. 'I came here with Hazel Ravenhair.'

The mouse looked shocked. 'But what about Santos?'

'I'm not her cat. We met in the forest, that's all.'

'But where *is* Santos?' asked the mouse.

'I've no idea,' said Beancat. 'I've never met him.' She thought for a moment. 'Hazel Ravenhair did say she feared for his safety.'

'I don't like this. I don't like this at all.'

'Us cats aren't like dogs,' said Beancat. 'We don't follow our special people everywhere!'

'I know that, silly,' said the mouse. 'Santos can look after himself. He's probably back at their home. I simply wondered how he'd feel about another cat getting all friendly with Hazel!'

'Do you know where they live?'

'In the village somewhere. Far too far for me to travel to, Hurly-Burly Beancat.'

Beancat suspected that the mouse had said her name wrong on purpose. 'It's

FURRY PURRY Beancat,' she corrected her. 'And you still haven't told me your name.'

'It is Velvet Pelt, Fleet of Paw,' said the mouse with obvious pride, 'but you can call me Vee!'

'Okay, Vee,' said Furry Purry Beancat. 'Seeing as how you're so chatty, maybe you could tell me a bit more about Agnes.'

'She's Hazel's aunt – her mother's sister – and was the local healer for years before her hands got too gnarly to mix the medicines. She taught Hazel all she knows.'

'Then isn't this place one of the first places the villagers will come looking for Hazel?'

'Why should they come looking?' asked Vee.

Beancat quickly outlined the previous day's events.

Vee gave a worried little squeak. 'Oh dear. That doesn't sound good at all.'

'And won't they come here?' asked Beancat.

'No,' said the mouse.

'How can you be so sure?'

'Because no one but Agnes and Hazel would dare venture this far into the forest,' said Vee. 'The villagers think it's haunted. No one even knows this house is here. The last lot stomping through the forest uninvited were the Roundhead soldiers, and they didn't find us.'

Hazel Ravenhair stirred in her sleep and rolled towards Beancat, who jumped

nimbly and silently to the earth floor. When she landed, she was stunned to find that Vee had jumped on her back.

What a cheek!

The mouse hopped off and sat herself by the leg of a stool. 'Why are you looking at me like that?' Vee asked.

'You really are—' Beancat was about to say the cheekiest, bravest mouse I have ever met, but then realized, of course, that

she had no IDEA how many mice she'd met in this and her other eight lives. She stopped and asked a question. 'Why are Cromwell's soldiers called Roundheads, do you know?'

'Of course I know,' said Velvet Pelt, Fleet of Paw.

'And are you going to tell me?' asked Beancat.

'Because of their shiny round-topped helmets, I suppose,' said Vee. 'So what are you going to do?'

'Do?' asked Beancat.

'Do,' said Vee. She licked both paws and gave herself a quick clean behind her ears.

'What do you mean "do"?' asked Furry Purry Beancat.

'You're going to help Hazel, aren't you?'

'She's not my special human . . .'

'You pets and your special humans. I'm a wild animal. I don't need a special human, but I care deeply for old Agnes and young Hazel.'

'I rather like being petted and pampered and loved,' said Furry Purry Beancat who, knowing how very beautiful she is, thinks she deserves it.

'So you're NOT going to help poor Hazel against the villagers and Silas Steele the witchfinder?'

'I didn't say that,' said Furry Purry Beancat. 'It's just that I'm not sure how I *can* help.'

Vee gave her tail a good clean while she

thought matters over. 'You could go to the village and find Santos. She's *his* special person and he'll want to help her *and* know what to do!'

'Now that's a good idea,' Beancat agreed. The truth be told, she'd been rather keen to meet Santos from the moment Hazel Ravenhair had mentioned him. She looked over to the latch on the door of Agnes's hovel. 'Do you know how to open the front door?'

'Of course I know!' said Vee indignantly. Her wetted paws were now cleaning her little tummy. 'You lift the latch.'

'I mean, *can* you do it?'

'What do I need a front door for? If I want to go outside, I go through a hole in the wall.'

'Is it big enough for me?' asked Furry Purry Beancat.

The mouse looked her up and down. 'If the hole were big enough for you, it'd be a window!'

At the mention of a window both turned to look at the one (glassless) window in the hut. There was an inside shutter across it with a crudely made hook holding it closed.

'If I stood on the table and you stood on my head, do you think you could lift the hook?' asked Beancat.

'I thought you didn't like being ridden like a horse?' said Vee.

'Without permission,' said Beancat. 'I'm *inviting* you on to my head.'

'Fair enough,' said Vee. 'I'll give it a go.'

So Velvet Pelt, Fleet of Paw climbed up on to Furry Purry Beancat's furry, purry back then up on to her head. Now Beancat jumped up on to the table and, with her front paws on the wall to steady her, stretched so that, up on her head, Vee was level with the hook.

The mouse heaved – and heaved – trying to lift the hook from above, then from below, like a strongman lifting weights.

'I've an idea,' said Beancat. 'You grip it from underneath and I'll push you from below with my head.'

'Let's go!' said the mouse. So she gripped and Beancat pushed and –

The hook came free from the eye (the metal loop in the frame) and the hatch swung open. Vee ducked and the bottom of the hatch just brushed the tip of Beancat's ears. That was a close shave!

'Excellent teamwork. I'll be off! No point in waking them.' Beancat nodded towards the sleeping women.

The mouse was already scuttling down the side of a table leg and back to the earth floor. 'Off you go, then. Good luck, Furry Purry Beancat!'

Beancat jumped up on to the window ledge. 'Thank you, Velvet Pelt, Fleet of Paw,' she said and, with that, jumped down to the forest floor and hurried away.

It was early morning and the birds were busy with the dawn chorus. Some sang warnings that there was a cat in the forest. Others shouted rude words directly at Beancat, either trying to warn her off or to attract her to them in an attempt to steer Beancat away from the more vulnerable young ones. Only a few birds were actually *singing* singing, because it was a beautiful sunny morning, they'd had plenty to eat and they were glad to be alive.

Beancat had no difficulty retracing her steps and then picking up the trail – in reverse – of where the villagers had been chasing Hazel Ravenhair into the forest. Follow it long enough, Beancat reasoned, and she should come to the village itself.

Passing what she thought of as 'Badger Tree', with one of the openings to the badger's underground home, she soon saw a small village in the distance: a church with a spire of wooden shingle tiles, a market square, an inn and a smattering of houses, most topped with the light straw colour of thatched roofing. There was one much grander house set back from all the others. It looked

newly built and its roof was of slate.

Another half-hour and she'd reached
the village. Everyone seemed to be awake
by now and preparing for the day. Shutters
were opening, steps being swept with just
the kind of broom Furry Purry Beancat
imagined a witch would ride – a bundle
of twigs wrapped round the bottom of a

wooden-pole handle – and buckets of water were being collected from a village pond fed by a fast-flowing narrow stream.

I think I'd like it here, thought Beancat, *if it weren't for the angry mob and talk of the witchfinder. I wonder if I live here in one of these houses with my special person?*

At that moment the church door opened and out stepped a man dressed from head to toe in black, with black buttons running all the way down from his neck to his ankles. On his head he wore an equally black hat with a brim so wide that Furry Purry Beancat was surprised that it fitted through the doorway. He was clutching a book in both hands and had such a serious expression on his face that he looked to

her like the kind of person who had never smiled in his entire life.

He must be the priest, thought Furry Purry Beancat. *His clothes are a kind of uniform.*

The priest peered down his pointy nose, straight at Beancat, who had stopped to look at him from the bottom of the churchyard path.

Have you noticed that cats are like that? If they want to stop and stare, even if it's IN THE MIDDLE OF THE ROAD, that's exactly what they'll do. If we humans want to be nosy, we have to be subtle about it, with a glance over the shoulder or a look in the reflection of a shop window. But cats? Cats just stop and stare like it's their right. And Furry Purry Beancat is very good at it.

'Begone, cat,' said the man in black. 'Shoo!' He gave a half-hearted wave of the arm.

You'll have to do better than that!

meowed Beancat, unimpressed.

'Begone!' said the man a second time, a slight quiver in his voice. He sounded to Beancat like a man who was raging inside and doing his very best not to explode.

He hates cats! she thought. *He really doesn't like us one bit.* So she promptly rubbed herself against his legs, purring as loudly as possible. This wasn't to try to make him like her, you understand. This was to get as much hair on to his black clothes as possible and to show him that she didn't care what he thought of her.

'Shoo!' the priest repeated.

Well, you're certainly not my special person! Beancat decided.

'Good morrow,' called a man from across the street.

'Good morrow, Master Farrow,' the priest replied. 'Are you, by any chance, on your way to see your brother John?'

'I am indeed, reverend. The poor soul. He is possessed!'

'Then I'll walk with you, if I may,' said the priest, 'for I intend to pray with him. The Lord willing, we can still save your brother from whatever evil enchantment that witch has put him under.'

This Master Farrow's brother must be Mucky John, thought Furry Purry Beancat. *From what poor Hazel Ravenhair told Agnes, it's his fever making him act this*

way. No magic spell! She was only trying to help him.

Furry Purry Beancat was tempted to follow Master Farrow and the priest – maybe even rub against his legs a few more times – but she was on a more important mission: to find Santos.

CHAPTER 4
SANTOS

Furry Purry Beancat decided to walk down the middle of the street, tail and head held high, to see if anyone called out her name and then she might find out where she belonged. At the same time she'd be on the lookout for Santos.

It wasn't a great plan. She'd only

trotted a few paces when she heard a cry of 'Witch's cat!', swiftly followed by 'It's the cat from the forest!' and 'It's Ravenhair's new familiar!', and before she could groan *'Oh no! Not AGAIN!'* an all-too-familiar boot went flying over her head.

Sure enough, when she dashed for cover, she was confronted by a charging mountain of a blacksmith with one shoe off and one shoe on, hobbling as before.

Furry Purry Beancat dashed round the back of the nearest cottage, over a hedge and into a field where she hid in the long grass by the edge.

'Who on earth are you?' asked a voice. In Cat.

Beancat nearly jumped out of her fur. She hadn't smelled another cat. She hadn't heard or sensed one either. It was almost as if he'd appeared out of nowhere.

She studied the cat next to her in the grass, still wet with morning dew. He was entirely black except for his thick white whiskers. He was obviously old and his legs were bony. But it was his eyes that caught her attention. They weren't green like hers but amber and very, very large

and round, almost too big for his head. And his tail. His tail was extraordinary. It was far longer than Beancat's, and like a black furry snake.

'Why, I'm Furry Purry Beancat,' said Furry Purry Beancat, trying to seem a lot cooler and calmer and more collected than

she felt. 'And who on earth are you?'

'I'm Santos,' said the black cat, though Beancat had guessed that already.

They both heard Thomas the blacksmith and few others shouting and stomping about in the near distance.

'Hazel Ravenhair is worried about you,' said Furry Purry Beancat. 'She's safe in the forest with Agnes.'

'That's a relief,' said the old black cat, his huge amber eyes looking deep into hers. 'And how do you know this, Mistress Beancat?'

'Because I've just come from there,' she explained. 'Do you know a mouse called – er – Velvet Fur, Fleet of Foot?'

'You mean Velvet Pelt, Fleet of Paw?' asked Santos.

'Didn't I just say that?'

'Almost,' grinned the old black cat, his impressive tail swishing on the ground. 'I know her well. She is the bravest of little creatures.'

'She thinks we need a plan.'

'She would,' said Santos. 'A plan for what?'

'For when the witchfinder comes,' said Beancat.

Santos slumped down on to his tummy. He suddenly looked even older. 'I knew it was only a matter of time before they called the witchfinder, once the king was beheaded.'

So I was right, thought Beancat. *This King Charles chap and his head did end up going separate ways.*

'Ever since then, everyone has been more and more mistrustful of each other. Friends turning on friends, families on families, family members on family members.' His thick white whiskers seemed to droop with sadness.

'So the Roundheads fight for this man

Cromwell and Parliament,' said Beancat, trying to remember all that had been said back in Agnes's forest home, 'but there are some still loyal to the dead king?'

Santos yawned. 'To the *new* king,' he corrected her. 'The king is dead, long live the king! How come you don't know all this already, Mistress Beancat? This news is three years old!'

'I'm not from these parts,' said Beancat.

Both cats' ears swivelled like satellite dishes to catch the sound of approaching footsteps. The form of Thomas the blacksmith loomed in front of them, but he was looking ahead and failed to spot the cats at his feet.

'The animal will have reached the forest

and run up a tree by now,' said his sister, Jane, the woman with the bird's-nest hair, reaching his side. 'It is only a cat. Let us get back to work.'

'Only a cat?' said the hulk of a man. 'A strange and beautiful one that none of us has laid eyes on before. If it is not that witch's familiar, I'll eat my hat!'

'You never wear a hat, brother,' said the woman. 'And that old Santos is her cat, remember. As dark as the witching hour on a starless night.'

The tip of her shoe was almost touching one of Beancat's white front paws.

Tom shuddered. 'The sooner Silas Steele gets here the better!' he said. 'He will put an end to this witchcraft.'

They, and a smattering of other villagers alerted to Beancat's arrival, soon gave up their search and returned to their morning routines.

Santos pulled himself to his feet and did a shuddering cat stretch, arched back and all. Beancat noticed flecks of grey hair amongst the black fur. She wondered just how old her new feline friend really was.

Furry Purry Beancat was stunned when she saw where Hazel lived. Having seen her Aunt Agnes's hovel in the forest and heard Hazel accused of witchcraft, she'd imagined Hazel Ravenhair living in a humble cottage, not this fine home!

'How come she lives in such a grand place?' she asked.

'This is Causely Hall, the home of Sir William Causely,' Santos explained as they skirted the village to reach the back of the house away from prying eyes. 'He also owns the land on which the village was built. Sir William was loyal to the king but, when he saw which way the wind was blowing—'

'Wind was blowing?'

'The way the war was going. He switched sides, swearing loyalty to Cromwell and to Parliament instead. He's kept the house but some villagers suspect he may still be a royalist at heart—'

'Still secretly loyal to the royal family . . . to the new king?'

'Yes, though the villagers should have no real complaints,' said Santos, jumping over a low box hedge into a small formal garden. Though old, with joints stiffened by age, the cat still made it look easy. 'Sir William has always been a fair landlord and a kind soul. He is Hazel's uncle. She's his late brother's child, so she's actually a Causely too.'

'Not Ravenhair, then?' asked Beancat.

'No,' said the black cat, 'Ravenhair is the name she took when she became the local healer. When her parents died, Sir William took her in. He treats her as he would his own daughter.'

Interesting, thought Furry Purry Beancat. *The man who owns this house is Hazel's*

uncle. It sounds as if he couldn't be more different to her Aunt Agnes. They must come from opposite sides of the family. She stored this away in her brain. 'And Sir William doesn't mind Hazel dabbling in all her herbal remedies?' she asked.

They had reached a half-open back door from which wafted wonderful cooking smells that curled their way up Santos's jet-black and Furry Purry Beancat's pink little noses. 'He didn't mind when the villagers welcomed her with open arms, helping mend broken bones, soothe fevers and bring down swelling.'

'But now things have turned bad for her?'

'With all this talk of witchcraft in the air,' said Santos, 'he's far less pleased. Things

88

have taken a nasty turn.'

Santos slipped inside the house, like a shadow moving with the sun, and Beancat was quick to follow. Her white furry tummy rumbled loudly. She'd had no IDEA how hungry she was until the delicious smell of food had woken her senses.

They padded through a small hallway into a kitchen where a youngish woman, wearing one of the now-familiar white caps, was hard at work.

'Greetings, Santos!' she said and, on spotting Beancat, added, 'and who is your beautiful lady cat friend?'

Beancat purred. She *liked* this woman. She liked her even more after both she and Santos were given a plate of food to share.

After Beancat had eaten, she explored the whole house with Santos and saw the various people who worked there, hiding from some – 'Don't trust the gardener,' Santos had warned her. 'He reports everything he sees and hears to the village.' – and making instant friendships with others. 'Jonas looks after the horses, and gives the *best* behind-the-ear scratches,' said Santos.

Jonas turned out to be an excellent cat-stroker and Furry Purry Beancat spent some quality time on his lap, letting him stroke her dark-striped back and purring like a train (not that they'd be invented for a good few years yet).

The cook's name was Bessy. 'After good Queen Bess,' Santos told Beancat.

'And did she lose her head too?' Beancat asked.

'No,' said Santos, looking confused. 'Queen Elizabeth died some fifty years ago. In her bed.'

'You seem to know a lot about kings and queens,' said Beancat. 'Are you a royalist, Santos?'

'I'm a cat,' said Santos, his amber eyes widening. 'My interest in Queen Bess is with the Spanish Armada.'

'And is this another thing I'm supposed to know about?' she asked. There seemed to be SO much she needed to understand in this one of her nine lives!

'No, but it is important to my personal history, Beancat,' Santos explained. 'An armada is a fleet of ships. In this instance it was a fleet of Spanish ships sent to invade England and seize Queen Bess's throne. My ancestor was a ship's cat on one of the Spanish fleet. The Spanish were defeated, their ships captured and she was brought ashore. Santos is a Spanish name. All my forefathers and mothers have Spanish names too!'

Furry Purry Beancat could hear pride in Santos's voice. There was extra fire in his eyes.

'Humans are a funny bunch,' she said. 'Country against country . . . royalist against Roundhead . . . villager against villager, with claims of being a witch. Your special human ISN'T a witch is she, Santos?'

'Of course not,' said Santos, but he turned as he answered so Beancat couldn't see his face as he spoke. 'And what if she were? If she *did* know any magic, she'd only use it to help others.'

Santos didn't just introduce Furry Purry Beancat to the people who lived and worked in the house but to some of its creatures too. There were the spiders who lived in the attic rooms. They were terribly polite and liked to keep themselves to themselves.

There was Bill, a very large rat with very large teeth, who was a friendly rival of Santos's. They liked to shout insults at each other and Santos made a show of chasing Bill when humans were about but – as long as the rat stayed out of the main house – the two remained friendly.

Then there was Crumbs. He was a mouse that lived in the house, which made things a little more complicated.

When Santos first introduced Furry Purry Beancat to him, he looked at her nervously.

'You're very, er, BIG, aren't you?' he said. He took a neat little nibble of a piece of cheese rind that he was clutching

in his two front paws.

'And furry,' agreed Beancat. She *purrrrrrred.*

'And purry,' observed the mouse. He ran his tiny needle-sharp teeth along the edge of the rind.

'Yes, she's all those things, Crumbs,' said Santos. He licked a front paw and rubbed it behind his own his ear. 'And she'll have the same deal with you that I do. As long as you and your family only come out at night – unless I call you – and never go in the kitchen, we can live together in peace and harmony.'

'If you say so,' said Crumbs. He was still a little unsure about Beancat.

'Do you know Velvet Pelt, Fleet of Paw?'
Beancat asked.

Crumbs stopped nibbling nervously and
he noticeably relaxed. 'She's a cousin of
mine!' he said.

'And a friend of mine,' said Beancat.

The mouse put down the cheese rind,
scuttled the short distance across the bare

wooden-planked floor and stood on his back legs directly in front of her, pulling himself to his full height. 'Then I'm very pleased to meet you,' he said.

There was a strong smell of mouse.

CHAPTER 5
WITCHFINDER!

It was the following day that Silas Steele the witchfinder arrived in the village and he did not travel alone. He brought with him an assistant and two soldiers dressed in the Roundhead uniform who, to both Beancat and Santos, smelled strongly of dog. Like the reverend, the

witchfinder was dressed from head to toe in black, with a short jacket, black breeches (trousers) and a black hat. The only flashes of colour were the large shiny buckles of polished silver on each shoe. His assistant, a somewhat thinner man – which is a polite way of saying that Steele himself was a little on the large side – was similarly dressed but with less fine shoes. He went by the name of Matthew Jones.

Much to Santos's disgust and Furry Purry Beancat's interest, he lodged at Sir William's house. Sir William had little or no say in the matter. To refuse him would suggest that he might have something to hide.

On arrival the two soldiers carried the witchfinder's trunk up to the bedchamber for the most important guests, and Matthew Jones scuttled up the stairs after them, ready to unpack his master's clothes. What none of the men noticed was a black cat slinking low and following them from a distance. The trunk delivered, the two soldiers came downstairs and out through the open front door. Silas Steele, meanwhile, had made his way into the main hall where Sir William awaited him.

Beancat sat in a corner in the shadows, watching and listening intently.

'Sir William,' said the witchfinder, with a curt nod of the head, 'I appreciate this

must be difficult for you: your own niece suspected of witchcraft—'

'I have no doubt you are a fair and honest man, Mr Steele,' said Sir William, getting to his feet, 'and that you will use your skills and expertise to find the truth. It is my firm belief that my niece, Hazel, is a good and God-fearing child and that the accusations of witchcraft are false.'

Beancat noticed that when Sir William said 'fair and honest' he stared at right into the witchfinder's eyes as if to say, '*You'd better be!*'

Beancat's nose, meanwhile, wrinkled in distaste. The witchfinder smelled *wrong*. Silas Steele smelled of . . . of pepper.

Yes, pepper.

What a strange and peppery man, she thought. *I'm sure I wouldn't have liked him even if he weren't here to make trouble for Santos's Hazel.*

Some half an hour later, the two cats met in the back garden, near a large muck heap. 'Steele has one other set of clothes, all black, which his assistant hung up in the wardrobe,' Santos reported. 'He had a Bible and a prayer book, some writing materials, and a drawstring bag that smelled of toad.'

'Toad?' said Beancat.

'Toad,' said Santos.

'Was it a live toad?' said Beancat.

'It smelled very much alive,' said Santos.

'And—'

'And?' asked Beancat.

'The bag moved,' said Santos.

'Did you talk to it?'

'No. I was snooping, remember? Trying not to be seen.'

'Yes, of course . . . Now what would Silas Steele be doing with a toad?' Furry Purry Beancat wondered aloud.

By listening to the witchfinder and his assistant's conversation with Sir William over a lunch of cold meats – which seemed to involve plenty of praying before, during, and after – Furry Purry Beancat gleaned plenty more information.

In turned out that the reason why Silas Steele had been able to come to the village

in just a matter of days, following Thomas the blacksmith's request, was because he had been in a nearby village.

'I was over in neighbouring Covington,' the witchfinder told Sir William. 'A Mistress Quint was believed to be a witch, and I conducted a series of tests and trials.'

Tests and trials? thought Beancat.

'Tests and trials?' asked Sir William.

The witchfinder nodded. 'I undertook a series of investigations at the end of which I conducted the final test. I will do the same here, with your niece.'

And what is the final test? Beancat wondered.

'And what is the final test?' asked Sir William.

'To have her thrown into their millpond,' said Silas Steele, almost matter-of-factly. 'If Quint floated to the top, she would have proved herself to be a witch and found guilty. As it was, she sank to the bottom, like a stone . . . so was, thus, proved innocent.'

Sir William was clearly upset. 'I thought

that this method was simply used to give troublesome folk a good soaking?' he said.

Beancat's beady cat's eyes caught the witchfinder trying to stop a cruel smile forming on his lips. A shudder went all the way down her furry body to the tip of her fluffy tail.

'It's a serious test, Sir William,' said Steele. 'I could see why Mistress Quint's neighbours suspected her of witchcraft, of course – and they were right to ask for my services – but she proved herself to be innocent of all charges.'

'But the poor woman was wrongly accused,' Sir William protested. '*Falsely* accused!'

The witchfinder's eyes flashed in anger and he gave his host a strange look. 'Falsely accused, Sir William? These are God-fearing folk who were worried for their very souls. It was their duty to call for me. Choose your words with care . . .'

If Sir William had been about to say something more, he was interrupted by the witchfinder's assistant, who had been eating silently beside Steele.

'Surely it is better that an innocent

person be wrongly punished than an evil witch be allowed to live, Sir William?' said Matthew Jones. 'Is that not so? We cannot have witches living among us!'

Sir William stopped his fork halfway between his plate and mouth.

Beancat was equally unhappy with what she was hearing. She'd been sitting quietly by the unlit fireplace, trying to attract as little attention as possible. She wasn't even sure if Sir William knew that she'd been in and out of the house these past few days. It was clear that he was fond

of cats, or of Santos, at least. She'd seen Sir William stroking and talking to the old black cat. Santos had later told her that he'd been talking about his niece, Hazel Ravenhair, hoping that she was somewhere safe and would stay hidden.

'I am shocked, sir!' said Sir William, now looking and sounding extremely worried. 'I believe my niece, Hazel, to be innocent of all charges and I am not sure your type of trial offers real justice—'

'Careful, Sir William,' said the witchfinder. 'I am here at the invitation of the villagers and with the full authority of Parliament.'

It sounded to Beancat almost like a threat.

'Your title is "witch*finder*", sir,' said Sir William, quick to steer the conversation in a different direction. 'Does that mean that you both find those you, yourself, suspect of witchcraft as well as find out whether those already suspected are witches or not?'

The witchfinder nodded. Unlike poor Sir William, worried for his niece, both Silas and his assistant had not lost their appetite for lunch, and he spoke with his mouth full. 'That is correct.'

'But in the case of my niece, Hazel, it's also a matter of your finding her first!' said Sir William.

'She is still missing?' asked Matthew Jones. 'The message my master received

was that they were hoping to have captured her before our arrival.'

'You arrived earlier than expected,' Sir William reminded them, 'and she has yet to be found.'

'Which rather suggests her guilt.'

'Which, Mr Steele, rather suggests she is in fear of her life and not, from what you've just told me, without reason,' Hazel's uncle pointed out.

'Have no fear about our finding her, Sir William,' said Matthew Jones. 'Whilst we have been enjoying your hospitality –' he gestured at the few cold meats that he and the witchfinder had not (yet) eaten – 'Larkins and Carstairs –'

'Our two soldiers,' said the witchfinder.

'– are out with Fang.'

'Fang?' said Sir William.

I don't like the sound of this, thought Beancat.

'My wolfhound,' said the witchfinder. 'I predict that Hazel Ravenhair will be my prisoner in a matter of hours.'

CHAPTER 6
PLODD

Furry Purry Beancat decided that if anyone knew the sort of tricks Witchfinder Silas Steele got up to, it would be the toad Santos had smelled in the drawstring bag.

It was with this in mind that Furry Purry Beancat slunk – cats are VERY

good at slinking – her way up the stairs and into the witchfinder's bedchamber.

'Pssst! Toad?' she said. 'Toad?'

There was a chair in the corner between the wardrobe and the window. On the seat was the black-velvet drawstring bag pulled tight shut. Wriggling.

'*Aw oo rufring tow mee?*' said a deep (and very muffled) voice from within.

Extraordinarily clever cat that Furry Purry Beancat is, she reached up and worked both her front paws into the tightly closed opening, pulling it wide. A large knobbly toad emerged, blinking in the light.

'Are you talking to me?' he repeated.

CROAK!

'Who else would I be talking to?' asked Beancat. 'Are there any other toads around here?'

The toad gave her *a look*.

If you've never been given *a look* by a toad you may not know quite what an effect it can have. When a toad gives you a

sideways stare with eyelids slightly closed, that look says, *What are you, some kind of an idiot?* even more strongly than if a room of people turned and pointed and shouted those words directly at you.

'I, er, don't know your name,' said Furry Purry Beancat, slightly flustered, which is *very* unusual for her.

'My name is Plodd,' said Plodd, in his deep toady voice. *CROAK.*

'And I'm Furry Purry Beancat.'

Plodd gave a deep-throated toady laugh that turned into a burp. *BUUUUURRRRRP!*

I'd have been embarrassed to make that noise, thought Beancat, *but it doesn't seem to bother him!*

'I'm hoping you may be able to help me,

Plodd,' she said.

'And why should I help you?' asked the toad. *CROAK.*

'Well, I did free you from that bag,' said Beancat.

'Maybe I like it in the bag. Toads like small dark spaces.'

'Do you?'

'Do I what?'

'Like it in the bag?'

'No,' said Plodd. *CROAK.*

'So.'

'So?'

'So will you help me?'

'Let me be clear on this. You only got me out of the bag so that I'd owe you a favour?' *CROAK.*

'No, Plodd. I got you out of the bag so that I could ask for your help.'

CROAK.

'Croak?'

'I'm thinking,' said Plodd. 'So you want me to help you because you want my help, not because I owe you a favour and have to help?'

'If you like,' said Furry Purry Beancat. 'If you want to see it that way.'

'I do,' said Plodd. 'I'm so sick of being MADE to do things.'

'By Silas Steele?'

'Yes.' *CROAK.* 'And the equally awful Matthew Jones.'

'Why do they carry you around with them?' asked Beancat. 'What does a

122

witchfinder need with a toad?'

'Do you know what a familiar is?' Plodd asked.

'Sort of,' said Furry Purry Beancat.

'It's supposed to be a demon disguised as an animal,' said Plodd. *CROAK.* 'It's like an evil helper for a witch, in animal form.'

'People call my friend Santos a witch's cat!'

'So they think he's her familiar,' said the toad. 'But it's not just cats. I've seen people accused of being witches for having a pig or a chicken or a goat or a cow—'

'But that's ridiculous!' Beancat protested. 'Most people round here work on farms. There are bound to be animals everywhere.'

123

Plodd gave her another one of his looks.

You know.

That look.

'Precisely,' he said. 'Silas Steele can claim just about any animal is a familiar, so can claim just about anyone is a witch.'

CROAK.

'That's terrible!' said Furry Purry Beancat.

'It is,' said the toad.

'But why do that?' asked Beancat. 'Why does the witchfinder go around the county claiming people are witches? It's such an awful thing to do.'

'I can think of plenty of reasons,' said Plodd, who'd had more than enough time to think, trapped in that bag for so many hours of the day, every day. 'These are dangerous times with half the people supporting the king and the other half Cromwell.' He gave a big *CROAK*. '"Witchfinder" sounds important, whoever's side you're on, so no one dares argue with him. Other people's fear of him keeps him safe. Then there's money. He gets paid for every witch he identifies. That's the agreement he makes with townsfolk and villagers *before* coming. And because there are no real witches –' if there were, Plodd hadn't seen any – 'he can decide how many he finds in a day.'

Furry Purry Beancat made a *HUMPH*-ing

sound, which is unusual, but not unheard of for a cat. The more she learned about Silas Steele, the less she liked him.

Plodd hopped forward on the chair. 'It would seem suspicious if the witchfinder condemned *every* person he investigated as a witch.' *CROAK*. 'But he still gets free food and lodgings wherever he goes. He and Matthew lead very comfortable lives.'

Beancat thought of the way they had devoured their lunch. Then she looked around the room. Sir William had certainly provided the witchfinder with very fine lodgings.

'Where do you fit into all this, Plodd?' she asked.

'Sometimes one of those accused of

witchcraft has no pet and doesn't keep animals,' he explained. *CROAK*. 'And – once they've sworn they have none – Matthew miraculously "finds" me, proving them to be a liar AND have a familiar.'

'That's a sneaky trick!' said Beancat.

'Not only that, there's something people find particularly loathsome about us toads . . .' said Plodd unhappily.

'Well, that's not fair!' said Furry Purry Beancat hurriedly. 'I think toads are very attractive and you're a particularly attractive one at that!'

Plodd gave a great big wide-mouthed toady smile. 'Thank you,' he said, followed by a great big toady *BUUUUUUUUURP!* 'I'm hungry.'

'Don't they feed you?'

'When they remember,' said Plodd. He now had a sad look in his toady eyes.

Furry Purry Beancat was silent for a while. She looked down at her two white front paws on the bedchamber rug, and thought.

'I have a plan for how we might be able to help Santos's special person if she's captured and accused of witchcraft,' she said, the cogs in her brain still whirring. 'It'll mean you getting back in the bag for now, I'm afraid. But if it all works out, someone should be visiting you tonight, when it's dark.' And, with that, she told Plodd her idea.

Beancat had not long been downstairs and back in the garden when news of Hazel Ravenhair's capture reached her. It came from a crow passing overhead, calling down to Santos.

'The witchfinder's men have your Hazel,' she cawed. 'They found her in the woods. Not the cottage. Agnes is safe. They are already returning!'

'Thank you, friend!' Santos called back up to her. He turned to Furry Purry Beancat. 'It's not just humans Hazel helps to heal,' he said. 'That was Israel. Hazel fixed her broken wing.'

Hazel Ravenhair was brought back to the village by the witchfinder's two soldiers. She walked between them, her long dark hair running down her back. One of the soldiers was holding an enormous dog, straining at the leash. Hazel strode between the two men, head held high.

People came out of their houses to watch. Some of them jeered and waved their fists. Others did the sign of the cross. Santos and Furry Purry Beancat watched from a distance.

The two soldiers walked Hazel up to the front of Sir William's house. The witchfinder, Silas Steele, opened the door as if he owned the place.

'Take her to the church and guard her overnight,' he ordered.

Sir William appeared at his side. 'Could you not keep her here overnight?' he suggested.

'Under house arrest?' Even from a distance Beancat could detect his concern for Hazel.

'And have her bewitch us in our beds?' said the witchfinder. 'I think not, Sir William!'

'But we don't even know if she *is* a witch!' Hazel's uncle protested.

'Not yet, we don't,' said Silas Steel. 'That is true. But we don't know that she's NOT a witch either. To the church.'

'Aye, sir,' said the soldiers.

The sour-faced priest wasn't thrilled at the prospect of his church being used as a prison, even for one night, but he understood the reasoning behind it. If Sir William's niece was a witch, her powers would be weakened in a house of God *and* the church was the securest building in the village because it was made of stone with thick oak doors. All of which could be locked. The soldiers and the dog would be in there with her too, making sure she

didn't get up to any mischief.

While the priest had been standing in the church porch making arrangements with the witchfinder's assistant, Beancat had been eavesdropping, rubbing against the priest who – you may recall – CLEARLY DIDN'T LIKE CATS. When she'd learned all she could from the two men's conversation, she walked away, leaving the reverend covered in fluffy Beancat hairs.

And so it was that Hazel Ravenhair spent her night in captivity in the church where her parents had married and she had been baptized. There was no way Santos and Furry Purry Beancat could get inside and, even if they had, there would have been Fang to deal with.

'He looks dumb, even for a dog,' said Santos.

'Tongue hanging out like someone falling out of bed,' agreed Furry Purry Beancat.

As you may have guessed, cats and dogs aren't generally friends.

When the sun went down, the two cats slunk into the churchyard – remember we talked earlier about just how slinky cats can be? – and Beancat jumped up gracefully on to a window ledge. A little less elegantly and a little more creakily, old Santos followed her. Now the two cats pressed their noses against the clear glass of the diamond-paned church window.

Through the distortion of the medieval glass, everything inside the church looked a bit wonky. Furry Purry Beancat blinked and tried to refocus her great big beautiful green cat's eyes. Candles lit the scene, and she could make out the figure of Hazel. She was sitting in one of the pews: a long, wooden bench.

Beancat tapped on the glass with a claw.

Hazel glanced up and looked in the direction of the window. It was dark outside, but she could clearly see two pairs of cats' eyes – one amber, one green – reflected in the candlelight. It was her beloved Santos and the newcomer, that beautiful furry, purry cat.

Her heart gave a little leap. The cats had come to see her and, although they wouldn't be able to DO anything, of course, the fact gave her some comfort and a warm feeling inside.

Little did Hazel Ravenhair know that Furry Purry Beancat planned to do a GREAT deal.

CHAPTER 7
THE TRIAL

The trial of Hazel Ravenhair was held on the village green next to the pond. All the villagers seemed to be there, including Thomas the blacksmith and his small band of followers. The priest was there too, and Sir William and most of his servants. The sun was shining and it was a beautiful day.

But not beautiful for someone accused of being a witch.

Everyone was standing in a big group until the witchfinder appeared with Matthew Jones at his side. They were quite a sight, what with Steele being so round and Jones so tall.

Behind the two men came Larkins and Carstairs, the soldiers, with Hazel between them, as before and, as before, she held her head high, proud and undefeated. Sir William looked at his niece and gave her a little smile and nod of encouragement.

Seeing Hazel being treated in that way, Santos – who was seated on his haunches next to Furry Purry Beancat on the branch of a tree – bristled. His hair became spiky

and Beany had no doubt that if he were a
dog, Santos would have launched himself
from the tree to attack the soldiers.

The crowd parted to form a circle, and
the witchfinder and his men walked to the
centre of it with the accused.

As far as Matthew Jones was concerned, Plodd the toad was safely hidden away in the drawstring bag in his coat pocket. But this was only partly true. Plodd was in the bag all right, and the bag was in his pocket. But safely? Not quite, for Beancat had been busy the day before.

After her conversation with Plodd, Furry Purry Beancat went looking for Crumbs the mouse again. She called a few times and heard scurrying in the walls but it took a while to tempt him to show himself.

'I know you're a friend of Velvet Pelt, Fleet of Paw,' said Crumbs, 'but you're still a cat and I'm still a mouse . . . and I have a very large family to look after!'

'Well, help me out tonight, Crumbs, and

I'll go to the kitchen and find something SPLENDID for you and your family to feast on for days. Maybe weeks, even!' said Furry Purry Beancat. THAT got his attention.

'What do you want me to do?' he asked.

'I noticed you nibbling that cheese rind.' said Beancat. 'I could see that you're a very neat nibbler.'

'I am a very neat nibbler indeed,' said Crumbs proudly. 'In truth I don't know a neater nibbler.'

'Good,' said Beancat, 'because I need you nibble a neat toad-sized hole along the bottom of a velvet drawstring bag.'

'You what?' asked the mouse. Of all the things he might have expected Furry Purry Beancat to ask him to do, it wasn't THAT.

'I need you to nibble a neat toad-sized hole along the bottom of a velvet drawstring bag.'

'I thought that's what you said.'

Beancat explained where to find Plodd and what to do. 'The most important thing – apart from being polite to Plodd and not getting caught, of course – is to make your nibbling as neat as possible, so no one spots any frayed edges or anything to give it away.'

'But if I neatly nibble a toad-sized hole in the bottom of the bag, isn't the toad going to fall right out?'

'That's why you've got to nibble the seam along the bottom. Unpick that thread with those tiny sharp nibbling teeth of yours, Crumbs,' Furry Purry Beancat explained. 'That way there'll still be folds inside the bag for Plodd to hold in that great big mouth of his, and he can keep the hole closed until he needs to get out. This requires a very skilful piece of nibbling,' Beancat added. 'That's why I've come to *you*, Crumbs. Don't let me down.'

Now, here at the witch trial, Matthew Jones thought that the toad was safely hidden away in the drawstring bag in his coat pocket when, in fact, Plodd had let himself out through the bottom of the bag and was free inside the pocket. The toad

was waiting for the next part of Furry Purry Beancat's plan.

'Gentle village folk,' the witchfinder began. 'We are gathered together for the most serious of reasons—'

'Amen!' the priest interrupted rather loudly and, feeling embarrassed, he looked down, only to see that he hadn't managed to brush off all Furry Purry Beancat's hairs from the day before.

Beancat and Santos had an excellent view of this and all other proceedings from up the tree.

'To determine whether a witch is living here in your community the trial will take three parts. The first being Testimony. The second, Evidence. The third, Trial by Water.'

And here was the challenge for Beancat, with a little help from her friends. She not only needed to find a way to show that Hazel wasn't a witch, but she also needed a way to stop the trial before things got out of hand. Beancat shuddered. She hate, hate, *hates* water.

'Who amongst you accuses Hazel Ravenhair of witchcraft?' demanded Silas Steele.

'I do, sire,' said Thomas the blacksmith, pulling himself up to his full height. 'When I asked her to marry me, she refused. Two days later, my smithy caught fire!'

'Witchcraft!' shouted the witchfinder's assistant.

'Asleep on the job again!' shouted a woman from the crowd. 'Not looking after the fire in your forge!'

'Silence!' boomed the witchfinder, with a voice of a man who was used to being listened to. 'Any other testimony?'

'Yes, sire,' said Michael Farrow, the man Furry Purry Beancat had seen greeting the priest when she'd first arrived in the village. 'I'm here on behalf of my brother John . . .'

That's Mucky John, the pig man, thought Furry Purry Beancat, remembering Hazel's

148

conversation with Agnes back in her woodland hovel.

'John himself is too ill to attend,' Michael Farrow continued. 'Hazel Ravenhair gave him a potion, and he had visions of the beast, and I fear he will not live.'

There was a big 'oooooooh!' of horror but – just moments later – it was followed by an even bigger 'OOOOH!' of surprise . . .

Real surprise. For who should be bounding towards them, alongside Sir William's horseman Jonas, but none other than Mucky John himself, looking as fit as a fiddle.

'Greetings, all!' he said, as he entered the circle, and the crowd hushed. 'What's going on here? Are you having revelries without

me?' Then he saw Hazel flanked on either side by the witchfinder's soldiers. 'What *are* you playin' at, Mistress Ravenhair? What games are these? Your potion worked a treat. My fever is sweated out; my dreams of my favourite sow, Miss Biggy, just

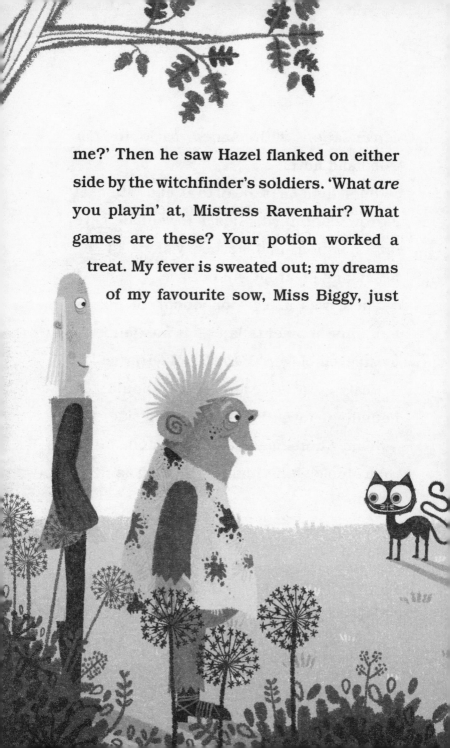

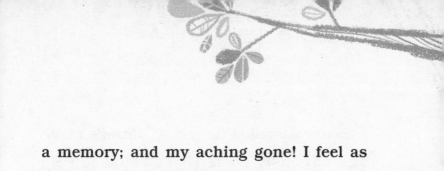

a memory; and my aching gone! I feel as young as a piglet! Thank you!'

Jonas, the horseman, nodded at his master Sir William, who nodded back.

Beancat smiled to herself. Hazel's uncle was obviously doing all he could to help her.

The witchfinder was clearly shocked but quickly regained control. 'I am sure your recovery was thanks to prayer, Mr Farrow, but I am glad to see you well. Now, who else has testimony against Mistress Ravenhair?'

A woman stepped forward. 'I did have a disagreement with Hazel Ravenhair and, when I came to milk my cow, the milk was sour!'

'Witchcraft!' shouted Matthew Jones.

'That rotten old bucket of yours, more like,' shouted another, causing a few ripples of laughter from the crowd.

'Silence!' shouted the witchfinder's assistant. 'More testimony!'

'One time, I had a cross word with Hazel Ravenhair and my donkey went lame!' said another.

'That donkey's been lame since the day it was born!' shouted a voice. There was more laughter.

Not everyone is against poor Hazel, thought Beancat.

'None of this is evidence against my niece,' Sir William protested.

'Careful what you say, Sir William,' said the witchfinder. 'For you may be found to have been harbouring a witch under your roof . . . and then there is the fact that some *men* are witches too!' He glared directly

into Sir William's eyes before turning back to the crowd. 'Sir William asks for evidence, which brings us to the second part of this trial: the presenting of the evidence.' He turned to Hazel. 'Do you have a cat?' he demanded.

Furry Purry Beancat glanced at her friend on the branch next to her. His amber eyes were on Hazel; his tail swishing.

'I do,' said Hazel.

'What do you call the beast?'

'I call my *cat* Santos.'

'And why choose a name so close to that of Satan or the Devil?'

'It is Spanish for *saint*!' said Hazel.

No one dared laugh now.

HA! thought Beancat.

'Saint?' said the witchfinder. 'This is blasphemy. Admit it. This is no ordinary cat! This is your familiar! A demon taking animal form!'

'Then why will half the village remember him as a kitten?' Hazel demanded. 'Ma Graham here owns the cat's mother and his grandmother too.' She pointed across the crowd.

An older woman tried to lose herself in the crowd.

'I remember the day I gave Hazel Santos as a kitten,' said Sir William.

Silas Steele's eyes narrowed. He was good at this game, at his trickery. He wasn't about to be beaten by these village *idiots*. 'Let us assume for now that this saintly

cat is just that. A cat,' said the witchfinder slyly. 'Do you have any other animals, Mistress Ravenhair?'

'Time for action,' said Furry Purry Beancat, jumping elegantly from the branch to the ground, while all eyes were on Santos's special person.

'No, I do not,' said Hazel.

'Not a toad?' asked the witchfinder.

'A toad?' said Hazel. 'What would I want with a toad, sire?'

At the first mention of the word 'toad', two things happened. Firstly, Furry Purry Beancat rubbed her furry, purry body against the left leg of Matthew Jones, the witchfinder's assistant, causing him to look down at her, missing the second

thing to happen: Plodd climbing out of the right-hand pocket of his coat, falling to the ground and hopping off in the grass.

'What indeed?' said the witchfinder. 'What would any God-fearing man or woman want with a toad? These repulsive beasts –'

Charming! thought Plodd as he plodded off. *You're not so handsome yourself . . .*

'– these *toads* cling to witches like a lamb clings to its mother! Find a toad and you'll find a witch. Find a witch and you'll find a toad!'

'Be quick, Plodd!' said Beancat from

behind the trunk of the tree, out of sight of the gathering. As the toad and cat had rehearsed the night before, Plodd clambered and hopped up Beancat's striped tail and on to her furry, purry striped back then head, just as Velvet Pelt, Fleet of Paw had climbed on to her head in Agnes's cottage.

'But I have no toad,' Hazel protested, 'so this is meaningless!'

'Then you will not mind being searched for one?'

'If you must,' said Hazel. 'If this will put an end to it.'

'And if we find a toad, you will admit you are a witch?'

'I will not because I am not,' said Hazel, holding her head high.

'Before I have my assistant search you,' said Silas Steele, 'I remind everyone that a toad in a person's possession is evidence enough of that person being a witch! Of consorting with evil.'

Beancat had no idea what 'consorting' meant, but it sounded impressive and the crowd obviously thought so too.

The witchfinder nodded to Matthew Jones, who stuck his hands in his coat pockets and strode towards Hazel Ravenhair. Only Furry Purry Beancat and Plodd saw the look of surprise then panic pass across the face of the witchfinder's assistant when he discovered that Plodd wasn't there. Jones kept walking but was glancing at the ground in case the toad had

somehow fallen out of his pocket. His plan had been to hide the toad in the palm of his hand and then 'discover' him in the folds of Hazel's clothes, as he'd done before.

But what now?

CHAPTER 8
THE PLAN IN ACTION

With the villagers watching him intently, the witchfinder's assistant couldn't very well NOT search Hazel Ravenhair but, then again, he couldn't warn Silas Steele that he wasn't about to 'find' a toad on her!

And, with all eyes on Matthew Jones, Beancat took the opportunity to trot

behind the witchfinder and raise her head with Plodd sitting between her beautiful tufty ears. The toad hopped on to the man's jacket. Beancat went back to the tree and jumped up and into it. She sat back down on the branch next to Santos, to keep a cat's-eye view on events as they unfolded.

'All done?' asked the black cat with the amber eyes.

'All done,' said Furry Purry Beancat. 'It's up to Plodd now.'

Plodd, meanwhile, had begun his long climb up Silas Steele's coat. The coat was thick and the toad was light, so the man didn't feel a thing. Unlike a frog, Plodd didn't have webbed feet or suction pads, neither of which would have helped him

climb this material. His feet were more claw-like and his grip was good.

Matthew Jones was busy pretending to search Hazel for a toad he knew wasn't there, because he couldn't put it on her in the first place! His face broke out into a sweat. This was *not* good.

'Anything?' asked the witchfinder impatiently. Jones was taking too long.

'N-nothing,' his assistant said at last.

'You're sure?' said the witchfinder, more than a little surprised.

The villagers turned to look at Silas Steele and gasped. And, let me tell you, a big bunch of people gasping together sounded like a single, mighty gasp:

GASP!

Hazel's uncle, Sir William Causely, stepped into the centre of the ring and the crowd hushed.

'Mr Steele,' he said, 'did you not say that, as well as a woman, a *man* can be a witch?'

'Indeed I did, sir,' said the witchfinder with a cruel stare.

'Did you also say that where you find a toad, you find a witch, and where you find a witch, you find a toad?'

'Yes, Sir William, I did,' said the witchfinder with growing impatience. 'But just because your niece does not have a toad, it does not mean that she *is not* a witch.'

'But having a toad would have been proof enough?'

'Yes.'

'But what if a toad had hopped on to her by chance?'

'Ridiculous! A toad is an aid to spells, enchantment and sorcery. It is evil, I say, sir. Evil!' said the witchfinder.

There were more gasps and mutterings from the crowd.

'Then,' said Sir William, 'perhaps you could explain to us why you have a toad on top of your hat?'

What is the man on about? the witchfinder wondered. He removed his hat and – to his horror – found . . .

No? What?

He had a toad on top of his hat.

Plodd looked at him. And burped:

'I, er, I mean, she must have . . . I . . . er
. . .'

'Witch!' shouted a lone voice in the
crowd.

'Witch!' shouted another.

Soon many voices were shouting 'witch'. But all were staring or pointing at the witchfinder, not Hazel.

'Silence!' commanded Steele, but no one was listening now. 'I am a man, not a witch!'

'But you said that men can be witches too,' Sir William reminded him, nice and loud so that the crowd would hear. 'Now let my niece go!'

Plodd took the opportunity to hop off to safety before anyone had the bright idea of trying to capture him. He timed it well because, a matter of minutes later, a large group of villagers had grabbed the witchfinder, Silas Steele, and the witchfinder's assistant, Matthew Jones, and were about to throw them in the village pond! They didn't come to any harm, but neither man survived with his dignity intact.

That afternoon Hazel went to visit Agnes in her hovel in the woods to tell her the good news, passing the badger's underground home along the way. Beancat came too. She was pleased to see the old woman again, and the old woman was pleased to see the two of them.

'Good riddance, I say!' said Agnes when Hazel had finished her report. 'Their days of accusing innocent women – and men – of witchcraft is over!

'Sir William sends his best regards,' said Hazel, perched on a three-legged stool, 'and asked me to remind you of his

open invitation to move into Causely Hall whenever you wish.'

Hazel's Aunt Agnes gave a snort. 'Can you imagine me living in a grand house in the village?' She laughed, looking around her tiny dwelling. 'This is my home. This is where I'm most comfortable. This is where I belong.'

Furry Purry Beancat went in search of Velvet Pelt, Fleet of Paw. She found the little mouse in a far corner, giving her snout a good clean with her front paws.

'I was wondering when I'd see you again,' said the mouse. 'Did you have anything to do with that toad ending up on the witchfinder's head by any chance?' She'd obviously been listening.

'What makes you think I might have had something to do with that, Vee?' Furry Purry Beancat asked in surprise.

The mouse stopped washing and looked at Beancat with a jet-black beady-eyed stare. 'Because toads aren't in the habit of sitting on top of the witchfinder's hat at just the right moment, I would imagine,' she said.

'I might have played my part,' said Furry Purry Beancat, 'but Plodd is the real hero—'

'Plodd?' said Velvet Fleet of Paw.

'The toad,' Beancat explained.

They heard the scraping of Hazel's stool as she got to her feet. 'I'll see you soon,' she said, kissing her aunt.

'Thank you for bringing me the news!' said the old woman. 'This is a great day.'

Beancat sauntered over to Hazel, her wonderfully fluffy tail held high.

'Are you coming with me or staying here?' asked Hazel.

Furry Purry Beancat answered by following her to the door. 'Goodbye, Velvet Pelt, Fleet of Paw!' she called out, though all the two people heard was a '*MEOW!*', of course. And neither heard the high-pitched squeak of the little mouse's reply.

Later that same day, Beancat and Hazel were back in Causely Hall with Santos on Hazel's lap. The old black cat was purring

almost as loudly as Beancat, that typical contented cat look on his face. Furry Purry Beancat lay curled up on a footstool opposite them.

Hazel spoke to her. 'I don't believe in magic,' she said. 'I believe in the power of nature and the healing power of plants, but not magic . . . so why do I believe your being here had something to do with my being saved?' She paused, scratching Santos between the ears. 'They called Santos here a witch's cat, but what are you, Mistress Cat?'

Beancat had been watching her through one open eye. Now she opened both and yawned.

'Whoever you are,' said Hazel, 'you are

welcome to stay here with me and my uncle, and Santos, for as long as you like. I must think of a name for you.'

I already have a name, she thought. *It's Furry Purry Beancat.*

Hazel frowned and thought a while. 'I have the perfect name,' she said at last. 'I shall call you Furry Purry Beancat!'

Beancat's beautiful green eyes widened. Her long white whiskers quivered. She had that feeling of butterflies in her stomach. *Does Hazel magically know my name?* she wondered. *Or* – and this is what made her feel so strange that her whole furry, purry body now tingled – *is this HOW I got my name? Did she give it to me? Is this – was this – the first of my nine lives?* Her purring reached maximum volume. *Perhaps you are a witch, after all,* she thought. *A good one!*

But, most importantly of all, Furry Purry Beancat knew she had found her special person.

With the day coming to a close and

the sun low in the sky, Beancat kept her promise to Crumbs and found the mouse some tasty morsels from the kitchen that should feed him and his family for a good while. She put them outside one of Crumbs's large mouseholes so he could pull them through.

'Thank you,' said Crumbs. 'You are a cat of your word.'

'And you are a mouse of yours,' said Beancat. 'You did some magnificently neat nibbling.'

'Thank you. You know, that warty, knobbly toad friend of yours may not be much to look at, but I rather like him,' said Crumbs.

'I expect a lady toad would find Plodd very

handsome,' said Beancat. *Though not as handsome as I am beautiful*, she thought, purring loudly. 'You may be pleased to know that Plodd's decided to live in the garden. Bill the rat has been given strict instructions not to lay a tooth or claw on him. I'm off to see him now, actually.'

'Goodbye, then,' said Crumbs. 'See you soon.'

'I hope so,' said Furry Purry Beancat. 'Who knows what tomorrow may bring?'

Once outside, it didn't take her long to sniff out Plodd.

'I think I'll like it here,' the toad announced. 'Though anywhere is better

than a bag.' *CROAK*.

'Good,' said Beancat. 'I don't let just *anyone* use me as a ladder, you know.'

'And I'm glad I'll no longer be used by those two to accuse innocent people of witchcraft!' said Plodd.

'Yes,' said Beancat. 'Your days of doing that are well and truly over. And so will theirs be when news spreads that the witchfinder condemned himself as a witch with his own words!'

BUUURRRRRP! burped Plodd happily, and he hopped off under a rock because that's what toads like to do. *CROAK*.

Furry Purry Beancat found a patch of sunlight, followed her tail round in a circle three times, then settled herself down in a

furry ball of purry cat. She yawned, lowered her head to the ground and pulled her beautiful fluffy tail in front of her little pink nose.

Where will I wake up next? she wondered, closing her big green eyes and drifting off to sleep . . .

PHILIP ARDAGH

Roald Dahl-Funny-Prize-winning author **PHILIP ARDAGH** has been published for around thirty years, written more than 100 titles and been translated into forty languages. Books range from his bestselling and international award-winning Eddie Dickens adventures — celebrating twenty years in 2020 — to his prize-winning Grubtown Tales, the Grunt series, illustrated by Axel Scheffler, and *High in the Clouds*, a collaboration with Sir Paul McCartney, currently being developed as a film by Netflix.

ROB BIDDULPH

ROB BIDDULPH is a bestselling and multi award-winning author/illustrator and was the official World Book Day Illustrator for 2020. His first picture book, *Blown Away*, won the Waterstones Children's Book Prize in 2015. His second book, *GRRRRR!* was nominated for the CILIP Greenaway Medal and the IBW Children's Picture Book of the Year in 2016.

DON'T MISS ALL THE ADVENTURES OF . . .

THE NINE LIVES OF
FURRY PURRY
BEANCAT

THE NINE LIVES OF
FURRY PURRY
BEANCAT

THE
RAILWAY
CAT

PHILIP ARDAGH

Illustrated by
Rob Biddulph

OUT
NOW!

THE NINE LIVES OF FURRY PURRY BEANCAT

PHILIP ARDAGH

Illustrated by
Rob Biddulph

THE LIBRARY CAT

OUT NOW!

THE REAL

FURRY PURRY BEANCAT

PHILIP ARDAGH didn't have a pet as a child, except when looking after the class tadpole one weekend. He was in his twenties when he got his very first pet, a long-haired tabby-and-white cat called Beany. 'I loved her to bits!' he said. 'She was very furry and very purry!' Beany lived into her eighteenth year and, in creaky old age, sat with Philip in his study as he wrote. One day, it occurred to him that – if he slightly skewed the meaning of a cat having nine lives – she could have

eight other exciting lives . . . and the idea of **THE NINE LIVES OF FURRY PURRY BEANCAT** was born.